MOONGOBBLE AND ME
THE DRAGON OF DOOM

Bruce Coville
ILLUSTRATED BY Katherine Coville

D0168875

SCHOLASTIC INC.
NEW YORK TORONTO LONDON AUCKLAND SYDNEY
MEXICO CITY NEW DELHI HONG KONG BUENOS AIRES

ISBN 0-439-79153-7

Text copyright © 2003 by Bruce Coville.
Illustrations copyright © 2003 by Katherine Coville. All rights reserved.
Published by Scholastic Inc., 557 Broadway, New York, NY 10012,
by arrangement with Aladdin Paperbacks, Simon & Schuster Children's
Publishing Division. SCHOLASTIC and associated logos are trademarks
and/or registered trademarks of Scholastic Inc.

12 11 10 9 8 7 6 5 4 3 2   5 6 7 8 9 10/0

Printed in the U.S.A.   40

First Scholastic printing, October 2005

Designed by Paula Winicur and Lucy Ruth Cummins

The text of this book was set in Historical Fell Type Roman.

The illustrations for this book were rendered in graphite.

MOONGOBBLE AND ME
THE DRAGON OF DOOM

For Jared Dietz

CONTENTS

MOONGOBBLE

RUSTY
KNIGHT

~◦ME, EDWARD◦~

URK

DRAGON

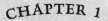

CHAPTER 1

THE COTTAGE ON THE HILL

I live in a little town called Pigbone.

Its full name is Pigbone-East-of-the-Mountains. I don't know if there is a Pigbone-West-of-the-Mountains. How could I? No one in our town ever goes anywhere.

"Why should we go somewhere else, Edward?" said my mother every time I complained about this. "We have everything we need right here."

I disagreed. What we didn't have was excitement.

Mother and I live in a little cottage at the edge of town.

Everyone in Pigbone lives in a cottage.

The only other kids in Pigbone are two older boys, who are kind of mean, and one new baby. So until Moongobble showed up, I sometimes got pretty lonely.

Behind our cottage is a big hill, very steep.

On top of the hill, right at the edge, sits another cottage, so big it's almost a house. It even has a kind of tower.

A long, twisty path winds up to this cottage, which had been empty for as long as I could remember. This cottage was where I went when I wanted to be alone. In fact, I spent so much time there I almost felt as if it belonged to me. So I was surprised, and a little upset, the day I saw smoke curling out of its chimney.

I ran to my mother.

"Someone has moved into the empty cottage!" I cried.

"Ignore it, Edward," she said. She wiped her hands on her apron and turned back to what she was cooking.

Mother was always cooking or washing or

something. Sometimes I could help. Sometimes she just wanted me to get out of the way.

I decided this was a good time to get out of the way.

I also decided that the most out-of-the-way place I could get was up the hill.

I started up the narrow path that led to the cottage. The grass beside the path was as high as my shoulders. Bugs buzzed around me. The sun was warm. I started to sweat.

When I was about halfway up the hill, I turned to look down at Pigbone. I counted the cottages. Fifteen, just like always. Our cottage was the closest. The one farthest away—the biggest and nicest one—belonged to the Rusty Knight.

I started to climb again.

I was out of breath by the time I got to the top.

I had planned to go right up to the cottage door and ask who was living there. Then I saw something that slowed me down. Bursts of green light were coming out of the window!

I decided to do some sneaking. This was something I had practiced a lot, so I was very good at it.

Dropping to my knees, I crawled toward the cottage. I moved very quietly.

As I got closer, I heard voices.

"You *know* that's not going to work," said one voice. It was deep and raspy.

"Don't be so gloomy!" said the other voice. It was softer and had a friendly sound.

"I'm not gloomy," said the first voice. "I'm honest."

I crept closer. Soon I was just beneath the window.

Vines covered the side of the cottage. Using the vines for support, I lifted my head to peek over the windowsill.

I couldn't believe what I saw!

CHAPTER 2

CHEESE!

Inside the cottage stood a pudgy old man. He was holding a smooth stick.

Bursts of green light were coming from the stick. *Magic!* I thought.

The man was wearing a brown robe and a soft hat. The hat was pointed. Two mice were sitting in the rim.

The mice and the man were staring at a big rock that sat on the table in front of him.

All that was odd enough.

6

Then I noticed something even odder. On the far side of the table, sitting in a little armchair, was the fattest toad I had ever seen.

He looked like a mudball with warts.

But even that wasn't the oddest thing.

The *oddest* thing was that the toad was talking!

"I really don't think you're ready for this," he said.

"Don't be silly!" said the man. "I have prepared the spell very carefully."

He pointed the smooth stick at the rock, then moved his left hand in a strange way. He began to hum. Suddenly he waved the stick and shouted, "Iggle! Biggle! Batzin Thebell. Free!"

A gust of wind blew past me.

A cloud of green smoke filled the room.

The man and the toad began to cough.

When the smoke cleared, I saw spatters of green goo every-where.

And the stone had turned into a piece of cheese!

Very ripe cheese, by the smell of it.

The mice began to cheer.

"Eeuw!" cried the toad. "That stinks!"

"Oh, bat barf," muttered the man. "The stone was supposed to turn into gold, not cheese!"

The toad hopped over to the cheese and sniffed at it. "Just as I told you!" it said, sounding cranky. "You used too much fizzlewort!"

"But why does it always have to be *cheese*?" groaned the man.

"Because you like cheese more than you like gold. Also, I think it has something to do with the way you make your *a* sound."

The mice giggled.

The toad glared at them. Then it said, "Anyway, before you worry too much about that spell, you should probably do something about the boy peeking through your window."

I jumped up and tried to run away, but something

grabbed my ankles. I crashed to the ground. Whatever was holding me got tighter. I looked at my feet. The cottage vines were tangled all around them. When I tried to crawl away, the vines started to climb my legs, moving like green snakes. The more I tried to escape, the tighter they got!

"Let me go!" I cried. *"Let me go!"*

The vines didn't let go.

I heard a slight cough. Looking up, I saw the magician standing in the doorway.

"Please!" I cried in horror. "Please don't turn me into cheese!"

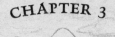

CHAPTER 3

MOONGOBBLE

The magician laughed. To my surprise, it was a nice laugh.

"Don't be silly," he said. "I'm not going to turn you into anything. But why were you spying on me?" He narrowed his eyes. "Did Fazwad send you?"

"I wasn't spying! I just came up to see who had moved into the cottage."

"Oh, let him go," said the toad, who was now sitting on the man's shoulder.

The magician stepped closer. Waving his wand,

he shouted, "Iggle! Biggle! Vinus Goletzim!"

Half the vines let go of my feet. But instead of sliding back to the cottage wall, they quickly wrapped around the old man's feet.

"Now you cut that out!" he cried.

The leaves shook a little, but the vines didn't move.

The toad rolled its big eyes. "I told you that guard spell was only half finished," it croaked.

The magician sighed. "Sorry," he said to me. "We'll have to wait for sunset. The vines will let go once it gets dark."

"What kind of guard spell doesn't work at night?" muttered the toad.

The magician ignored him. "My name is Moongobble," he said. Nodding toward his shoulder, he added, "And this is my friend, Urk."

"I'm Edward," I said.

Moongobble reached down and helped me to my feet.

Waiting for sundown gave us time to get to know each other. I told Moongobble about life in Pigbone. This didn't take long. Then I said, "Why did you decide to move here?"

"I needed a quiet place to practice my magic," he answered.

"He needs a *lot* of practice," added Urk.

This surprised me. Moongobble looked as if he had already had a long time to learn magic.

"Are you new at this?" I asked.

He smiled happily. "Quite new! I've only been doing magic for two years."

I thought this was very odd. Every grown-up I knew had had the same job for his whole life.

"What made you decide to become a magician?" I asked.

Moongobble smiled. "Well, I used to be a shoemaker. I was having a hard time of it until a group of elves started to help me out. They did it in secret, of course. But I spied on them a few times. They were the ones who got me interested in magic. In fact, after a while, magic was all I could think about. The elves had been so good to me that I had enough money to live on. So I decided to close my shop and become a magician. I want to be the best magician ever!"

"You've got a long way to go," muttered Urk.

The mice in Moongobble's hat giggled. I noticed

now that there was a little door that they used to go in and out.

I liked Moongobble.

I wasn't sure how I felt about Urk.

The sun began to set. The shadow of the mountains stretched over us. Fireflies came out, moving around us like little lost stars.

"The vines will let go soon," said Moongobble softly. He sounded almost sad. After a moment he said, "How would you like to be my helper, Edward?"

"Would I get to learn magic?" I asked excitedly.

Moongobble shook his head. "You must be an apprentice to learn magic. And I can't have an apprentice until—well, I can't have an apprentice yet."

"Then what would I do?"

"You could help me gather things I need for spells. We would have to go on trips, of course. We would go into the deep woods. Sometimes we would go into caves. It might be scary."

"I would love that!" I shouted. Then I sighed. "I'll have to ask Mother though. I don't know if she will let me."

"It's a paying job," said Moongobble. "A silver penny every day."

I blinked. A penny was a lot of money in Pigbone and Mother and I were very poor. "That's different. Mother might say yes if I tell her that."

Something tickled my ankles. I looked down. The vines were letting go of my feet.

"I have to hurry home," I said, once I was free. "Mother is going to be angry with me for being so late!"

"Come back soon!" said Moongobble.

"I'll try!" I called.

I *had* to convince Mother to let me work for Moongobble!

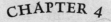

CHAPTER 4

HELPING MOONGOBBLE

Just as I expected, Mother was angry when I got home.

"Where have you been, Edward?" she asked.

"Wait until you hear! There is a magician on the hill. He wants me to be his helper! He'll pay me a silver penny every day!"

Mother stared at me. "Are you making this up?"

"No, it's true, it's true! Oh, please let me do it."

Mother scowled. "I want to meet this magician before I say yes," she said.

The next morning we climbed the hill to Moongobble's cottage, carrying some of Mother's freshly baked bread. Mother says you should always bring bread to a new neighbor. I had not known this, mostly because Moongobble was the first new neighbor we had ever had.

Urk was squatting outside the cottage door. "Good morning!" he croaked.

Mother grabbed my arm. "Did that toad just talk?" she whispered.

Urk rolled his eyes. "Why do people think a talking toad is so unusual?" he asked.

"Because most toads don't do it!" said Mother. She looked at him sternly. "Did you used to be a prince or something?"

Urk made a face. "No, madam, I did *not* used to be a prince. And if you kiss me, I will not turn into anything besides what I am right now. So don't even think about it."

"The thought never crossed my mind," said Mother. "We are here to see Moongobble."

"He's inside," said Urk, pointing to the door.

We went in. Moongobble was sitting at the table, piling apples one on top of another. He had a pile eight high, which I thought was amazing.

"I'm studying balance," he said, not even looking at us. "A magician must understand the balance of the universe."

One of the mice in his hat sneezed. The pile of apples wobbled, then fell down.

Moongobble sighed. "Oh, well," he said. Then he stood and turned to us. "Ah, you must be Edward's mother. I am very glad to meet you."

Mother and Moongobble talked for a while.

Please say yes, I thought. *Please. PLEASE!*

Mother asked Moongobble many questions about what he wanted me to do. She listened very carefully, and did not smile at all. So I was surprised when at last she said, "All right, I will let Edward work for you."

I couldn't believe it. I was going to be a magician's helper!

Moongobble and Mother shook hands. "I will take good care of your boy, madam," he said. "Magician's honor!"

"You'd better," she said sternly. "And I expect you to pay him every day."

After Mother had gone, Moongobble took a pair of baskets from the wall and said, "Come on, Edward. You can help me gather things for spells."

I followed Moongobble out of the cottage. Urk hopped along beside us. We walked around the cottage and into the woods.

I had never entered these woods before. They are deep and dark and spooky. People say strange things live there.

I tried not to be frightened.

After a while we came to a little stream.

"Stop!" said Urk, who was now riding on Moongobble's shoulder. "Try that tree, right there. The big one."

Moongobble knelt beside the tree. It was so big I could not have put my arms even halfway around it.

Slowly, carefully, he lifted away dead leaves. "Silver whistlewort!" he cried. "You are a genius, Urk!"

"I know," croaked the toad happily.

Moongobble showed me how to recognize the plant. Its leaves were white and fuzzy, and it had a sharp, spicy smell. We had to go to many trees, but by lunchtime our baskets were half full.

"What do you use this stuff for?" I asked, trying to wipe the smell off my hands.

Moongobble closed his eyes. He appeared to be thinking very hard. "Silver whistlewort is good for healing potions, love potions, and spells of disguise," he recited. "You can mix it with unicorn water to make a spell of invisibility. It is also good for getting rid of werewolves."

"But *he'll* mostly use it to turn things into cheese," said Urk.

Moongobble stuck out his tongue.

The talk of cheese made us hungry, so we took out our lunch. We had the bread Mother had sent with me. We had firm, sweet apples. And, of course, we had cheese.

It was a very good day.

The next day and the next were much like this one. We went deep into caves. We waded through swamps. We climbed tall trees.

I had never been so happy.

Then one morning I came to the cottage and saw that Moongobble was very upset.

Urk was upset.

Even the mice in Moongobble's hat were upset.

"What's wrong?" I cried.

CHAPTER 5

A PROBLEM

Urk pointed to a bat hanging from the edge of the table. "Flitbert here just brought some bad news."

"Don't blame me!" squeaked the bat. "I don't *make* the news. I just deliver it."

"What *is* the news?" I asked.

Moongobble sighed. "Fazwad is coming."

It was the first time I ever heard him sound gloomy.

I remembered that he had said that name before.

"Who is Fazwad?" I asked.

"His full name is Fazwad the Mighty," croaked Urk. "He's head of the Society of Magicians."

Moongobble sighed again. "Fazwad does not think I am a very good magician."

"You aren't a very good magician," said Urk.

"In my heart I am!" cried Moongobble.

"And you have a very good heart," said Urk. "But a good heart and hard work are not enough for Fazwad. He wants you to *be* a good magician."

"I just need more time!"

"That's all very well," said Urk. "But if you want to do magic in this kingdom, you must be a member of the Society of Magicians. It's the law."

"Why don't you just join the society?" I asked.

"It's not that simple," said Moongobble. "First I have to prove I am good enough."

"Which is why Fazwad is coming to inspect him," said Flitbert, who was still hanging from the edge of the table. "He wants to see how good Moongobble's magic is."

"And if I *can't* prove I am good enough, they won't let me in," said Moongobble.

"Uh-oh," I said, thinking of all the spells I had

seen go wrong over the last few days.

"Precisely," said Urk.

Moongobble sighed. "I knew this would happen someday. But I hoped I would have more time to practice first."

Now I understood why everyone looked upset. I was upset too. If Fazwad made Moongobble stop being a magician, he might leave the cottage.

I would lose my job.

I would lose my chance to make money.

Worst of all, I would lose my only friend.

"When is Fazwad coming?" I asked.

"Two days," said Flitbert.

"I'll help you get ready," I said. "What do we need to do?"

"Moongobble must have three spells to show," said Urk. "Also, we must clean the cottage. I know Fazwad, and he is very fussy."

The cottage looked fine to me. Books were piled everywhere of course, and there were stacks of things for Moongobble's spells. But I liked it that way.

"We'd better get busy," said Urk. "Moongobble, you go practice. Edward and I will take care of the mess."

MAGICAL
PROPERTIES
of the
DUNG-
BEETLE

As it turned out, toads are not built to do housework, so I was the one who took care of the mess. I put the books on shelves, except one that Urk kept to read. I packed the spell stuff in boxes. I scrubbed and cleaned.

Moongobble tried using magic to help, but when he cast a spell on the broom, it ran out the door crying, "Mommy, Mommy!" When he tried to fill the mop bucket by magic, he caused a small flood. And when he tried to call up a wind to blow the dust out the window, it made the room smell like a giant fart.

"Oh, just go practice," said Urk, holding his nose. Then he turned back to his book.

By noon of the second day the cottage was bright and shiny.

We went to sit outside to rest for a bit.

"Let me show you my spells," said Moongobble proudly.

But before he could start, we heard a buzzing sound. Suddenly a man was standing in front of us.

"Uh-oh," said Urk.

"Welcome, O Mighty Fazwad," said Moongobble.

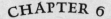

CHAPTER 6

FAZWAD THE MIGHTY

Fazwad had dark eyes that seemed to look into corners that weren't even there.

He looked at Moongobble and sniffed, as if he were smelling something bad. "Are you ready to show what you can do?" he asked.

Then he sniffed again.

"I'm ready," said Moongobble, trying to sound cheerful.

I noticed that the mice had gone back inside his hat.

We went into the cottage.

"Have a seat," said Moongobble, pointing to the big chair.

But when Fazwad tried to sit down, the chair yelped and ran away. Fazwad landed on his bottom. He did *not* look happy.

"I am *so* sorry!" cried Moongobble. He turned to the chair. "Chair!" he yelled, shaking his wand at it. "You get right back here!"

The chair walked slowly back to Fazwad. It whimpered as it came.

I didn't blame it. I wouldn't want Fazwad to sit on me, either.

"Oh, never mind," said Fazwad. "Just show me what you can do."

For his first trick, Moongobble pulled a mouse out of his hat.

Fazwad yawned.

For his second trick, Moongobble made the mouse vanish.

Fazwad looked as if he were going to fall asleep.

"Let's see some real magic," he said.

"All right!" said Moongobble. "Watch this!"

He put a stone on the table.

"Oh, no," whispered Urk. "Not that one!" He covered his eyes. "Tell me when it's over, Edward."

Moongobble shook his wand at the stone. He muttered some words. A gust of wind blew past me. A cloud of green smoke filled the room.

When the smoke cleared, we saw the stone had become a piece of blue cheese. Green goo was spattered everywhere.

Most of the goo was on Fazwad.

"That does it!" he roared. "The Society of

Magicians has no use for fools like you, Moongobble! I hereby forbid you to practice magic in this kingdom!"

"Please!" I cried. "Give him another chance!"

"Why should I?" sneered Fazwad.

"Because the rules say you must," said Urk. "Society of Magicians Handbook, page thirty-eight. You can look it up. I did."

Fazwad glared at Urk. Then he nodded and said, "The toad is right. If you fail your test, it is still possible to join the society by performing three Mighty Tasks."

To my surprise, he started to smile.

I did not like the way Fazwad looked when he smiled.

"So here is your first task: You must fetch me the Golden Acorns of Alcoona!"

Moongobble gasped. "But . . . but . . ."

"Do you want to be a magician?" growled Fazwad.

Moongobble nodded, still trying to talk.

"Then get me those acorns! You've got three days!"

Fazwad flung his cape around him, sniffed twice,

then vanished in a puff of blue smoke.

It did not leave spatters of goo behind it.

"What am I going to do?" groaned Moongobble.

"I'd suggest you fetch those acorns," said Urk.

"You don't understand," said Moongobble. "The Golden Acorns of Alcoona are guarded by a deadly dragon."

None of us said anything for a little while. Finally I asked, "Just how deadly is this dragon?"

Moongobble shivered. "They call it . . . the 'Dragon of Doom.'"

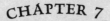

CHAPTER 7

THE RUSTY KNIGHT

Moongobble and I were sitting at the table.

Urk was sitting *on* the table. Pointing at Moongobble, he said, "Dragon of Doom or not, if you want to be a magician, you must fetch those acorns."

"I know, I know," said Moongobble with a sigh. He slumped back in his big chair, which did not run away from him. "But how?"

"I'll help!" I said eagerly.

I didn't know what good I could do against a

dragon, but this sounded like a great adventure.

"I'll help too," said Urk.

He did not sound happy about the idea.

"Thank you, friends," said Moongobble. "But I cannot ask you to go into danger like this."

Urk rolled his big eyes. "Don't be silly, Moongobble. What are friends for? Now, who else can we get to help?"

"I know!" I cried. "We could ask the Rusty Knight."

"Who is the Rusty Knight?" asked Moongobble.

"He lives at the far end of Pigbone. He's not really a knight anymore. But he used to be."

"Why isn't he a knight anymore?" asked Urk.

"He told me he had one joust too many and now he always has a ringing in his ears from being whacked on the head so many times. He's a nice man, but kind of strange."

"I know the type," said Urk, glancing at Moongobble.

"Do you really think he would help us?" asked Moongobble.

"It can't hurt to ask," I said.

"Then let's go ask!" said Moongobble.

We started out the door. Chair tried to follow.

"You go right back inside!" said Moongobble sternly.

Chair whimpered, but did as Moongobble said.

I was impressed.

We walked down the hill, past my cottage, straight to the home of the Rusty Knight. His cottage had a big flower garden in front, with lots of roses. Its walls were covered with ivy. And it had a real glass window, the only one in Pigbone.

As we got closer, we heard weird squeaking and clanking sounds from inside.

Moongobble knocked on the door.

No one answered.

"Knock harder," I said. "Maybe he didn't hear you."

This time Moongobble pounded on the door.

"Just a minute!" called a voice. We heard more clanking and squeaking. Then the door swung slowly open to reveal an old man dressed from head to toe in rusty armor.

"Well, at least we know how he got his name,"

muttered Urk, who was sitting on my shoulder.

"Hello, Edward," said the Rusty Knight cheerfully. "I was just trying on the old suit to see if it still fits." He raised his arm, which made a dreadful squeak. "Needs oiling," he said. "Who are your friends?"

I introduced Moongobble and Urk, which I had to shout to do. Then Moongobble said, "We go to face a mighty dragon. We are hoping you will join us."

"A mighty *what*?" asked the Rusty Knight. He tried cupping his hand to his ear, but his helmet got in the way.

"Dragon," said Moongobble, speaking very clearly.

The Rusty Knight looked surprised. "But that's a job for a knight!" he said.

"You *are* a knight," I pointed out.

He blinked. "Well, yes, of course I am.

But I haven't done anything knightly for a long time."

"We really do need you," I shouted. "Moongobble has to fetch a treasure that's guarded by the Dragon of Doom."

"Dragon of Gloom?" asked the Rusty Knight, looking puzzled.

"Doom!" bellowed Urk. "Dragon of *Doom*!"

The Rusty Knight looked at Urk. "Ah, a talking toad! Reminds me of the old days. So, you have to face the Dragon of *Doom*?" He gazed into the distance for a while. Then he smiled and said, "I cannot move as fast as I used to. And my hearing is not very good. And I squeak a lot. But I'll come if you really want me to."

"We do," I said.

"All right. Help me finish oiling my armor and we'll be on our way."

But I knew we would not be on our way just yet.

First we had to talk to my mother.

I knew she was not going to like this idea.

I also knew I would just die if I didn't get to go along!

CHAPTER 8

GETTING READY

I would have liked to put off talking to Mother. But to get from the Rusty Knight's cottage to Moongobble's cottage we had to walk back past my front door.

"Ah," said Urk as we did. "We should talk to Edward's mother while we're here."

It was the first time I ever wanted to strangle a toad.

Mother was making bread. She was glad to see Moongobble because the silver pennies I had been bringing home had made our life much easier.

Moongobble made a deep bow. Then he said, "We are off on a quest tomorrow. I would like for Edward to join us."

Mother wiped her hands on her apron. "Will you be gone long?" she asked.

"With luck we will be home by Tuesday," said Moongobble.

Mother nodded. "Will it be dangerous?" she asked.

Moongobble frowned. "I cannot lie to you, madam. It may be dangerous for me."

"And me," said the Rusty Knight. "Because of the bath water."

My mother knew the Rusty Knight well enough not to ask what he was talking about.

"But Edward is coming simply as a helper," said Moongobble quickly. "So he should not get anywhere near the dragon."

"*Dragon?*" gasped Mother.

"The Dragon of Doom, to be specific," said Moongobble. "But I repeat: Edward should not get anywhere near it." He lowered his head. "To tell you the truth, I would like to have someone along to bring back the news should I perish."

Mother took a deep breath. Then she said, "Do you promise to take good care of Edward? *All* of you?"

Urk lifted his front right foot and put it on his chest. "On my honor as a toad," he said.

"On my honor as a knight," said the Rusty Knight.

"On my honor as a magician," said Moongobble.

I wasn't sure if this counted, since Moongobble wasn't really a magician yet. But it seemed to work for Mother.

"All right," she said. "Edward can go."

I threw my arms around her waist. "Thank you!" I cried. "*Thank you!*"

The next morning I got up very early. On the table I found a bundle of food that Mother had prepared. I slung it over my shoulder and started up the hill to Moongobble's cottage.

The grass was still wet with dew.

The world smelled fresh and clean.

I felt happy, and excited.

I heard something clanking and creaking behind me. Turning, I saw the Rusty Knight hurrying to catch up with me. He couldn't hurry very well though.

"Good morning, Edward," he said when he was by my side. "Hail and well met!"

"Hail and well met," I replied loudly.

It seemed like a grown-up way to talk.

"Nice day for an adventure, isn't it?" said the Rusty Knight.

"I was just thinking the same thing," I said.

"Glad your nose is feeling better," he said.

I didn't try to figure out what he was talking about. Moongobble was waiting, and we had an adventure to begin.

CHAPTER 9

THE DRAGON'S CAVE

We found Moongobble standing at the bookshelf. The pockets of his robe were bulging with slips of paper. More papers were tucked into his belt.

Urk was sitting on a shelf, in a gap between some books. "Edward and the Rusty Knight are here," he said.

"Wonderful!" cried Moongobble. He turned and smiled at us. "I'm almost ready. Edward, come write some things down for me, would you?"

I stood behind him as he read off a spell.

"If we're lucky, he'll turn the dragon into cheese and that will be the end of it," muttered Urk.

"Fleas!" cried the Rusty Knight, who had come over to watch. "I like that idea. We'll get the dragon while he's scratching!"

"Cheese!" shouted Urk. "*Cheese!*"

Moongobble had me copy two more spells, then said, "That's it. I'm ready to go."

"You forgot the map," said Urk.

"Drat," said Moongobble. He picked up another piece of paper and crammed it into his pocket with the others.

As we left the cottage Moongobble bent toward the vines and whispered, "We'll be back soon. Please guard our home well."

Urk rolled his eyes, but said nothing.

We entered the forest. Even though it was a bright morning, the trees blocked the sun. A low mist still covered the ground.

Moongobble looked at the map every once in a while. "Turn here," he would say, or, "Wait, we need to go back!"

Soon we turned away from the paths I knew. Before long we were walking past trees bigger than any I had ever seen. Most of those trees had holes in their trunks, and from most of the holes bright eyes watched carefully as we walked by.

We came to a stream. I took off my shoes to wade across. The cool water felt good against my feet.

A little while later we walked along the edge of a cliff. I tried not to look down. It was a long way to the bottom.

Then we were back in deep forest.

"I think we're lost," said Urk after a while.

"Why do you say that?" asked Moongobble. He sounded worried and a little cranky.

"Because we just passed that same fallen tree for the third time," shouted Urk.

"I thought it looked familiar!" cried the Rusty Knight happily.

"Now what do we do?" I asked.

"Take another look at the map," said Urk.

"What an excellent idea," said the Rusty Knight. "I'd love a nap."

"Map!" bellowed Urk. "Study the *map*!"

"Oh!" said the Rusty Knight. "Sorry, didn't quite get that. I used to be quite good with maps. Let me take a look."

Grumbling a little, Moongobble handed him the map.

The Rusty Knight studied the map carefully. After a moment he cried, "Aha! Here's the problem. You were holding it upside down!"

Moongobble turned red. The mice in his hat giggled.

We began to walk again.

Late in the day I smelled something strange.

"What's that?" I asked.

"Smoke," said Urk. "Moongobble, are you doing another spell?"

"It's not me," said Moongobble.

"Then it must be the dragon!" said the Rusty Knight. He sniffed the air. "Yes, that's dragon smoke. I'd know it anywhere. We must be near his cave."

We walked more slowly now.

"Look!" whispered the Rusty Knight. "*There it is!*"

Ahead of us was a clearing.

On the far side of the clearing rose a rocky cliff.

In the center of the cliff was the dark mouth of a cave.

From the mouth of the cave curled wisps of smoke.

No doubt about it.

We had found the Dragon of Doom!

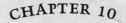

CHAPTER 10

ANOTHER MISTAKE

"I need to get closer," said Moongobble.

"We can't go straight across the clearing," I said. "We should sneak around the edge."

Moongobble shook his head. "*We* are not going to the cave, Edward. From here on I must go alone."

"But—"

"I promised your mother," said Moongobble sternly.

"Oh, all right," I said, feeling grumpy.

"Surely, *I* must come with you," said the Rusty Knight.

Moongobble shook his head. "No, you must stay here to protect Edward and Urk."

"Gee, thanks," muttered Urk.

Moongobble started forward. He had not gone far when he stepped on a twig. It made a loud snap.

"Uh-oh," said Urk.

We heard a mighty roar. Then a huge ball of fire shot out from the cave.

The fire vanished, leaving a cloud of heavy smoke.

More light came from the cave. The light cast a shadow on the smoke—the shadow of a dragon.

We could see the shadow of its pointy wings.

We could see the shadow of its sharp teeth.

And we could see that it was huge!

"Hmmm," said Moongobble. "This is going to take some serious magic."

"Are you kidding?" croaked Urk. "This is going to take some serious running away!"

"Perhaps I can lop off its head," said the Rusty Knight, tugging at his sword. It was stuck, and he had to tug several times before it came out of its scabbard. When it finally did come loose it made a horrible squeal. Holding up the blade, the Rusty Knight began clanking forward.

"Stop!" called Moongobble. "This is my job!"

The Rusty Knight stopped. He looked puzzled.

"You must protect the others," said Moongobble again. "I must deal with the dragon."

He rolled up his sleeves. Then he pulled a handful of spells out of his pocket and sorted through them. "Aha," he said, holding up a paper. "This should do the trick."

Urk put his front feet over his eyes. "Tell me when it's over," he groaned.

Moongobble walked to the center of the clearing. He tossed a handful of shiny powder into the air. Waving his wand, he cried, "Iggle! Biggle! Furball!"

Thunder split the sky and a bolt of lightning sizzled into the clearing.

When the smoke cleared, green goo was spattered everywhere.

But Moongobble was gone.

Where he had been standing was a big chunk of cheese.

Blue cheese.

Wearing a hat.

"He's finally done it," groaned Urk. "He's turned *himself* into cheese! I knew it would happen someday."

The mice had climbed out of Moongobble's hat. They were looking down at the cheese, squeaking in a puzzled way.

"For heaven's sake, don't eat it!" cried Urk.

The mice scampered back inside the hat.

"Looks like toasted cheese for the dragon tonight," said Urk sadly.

I couldn't let that happen! I was afraid the dragon might toast me instead. But I couldn't just leave Moongobble there for him to eat. So I rushed into the clearing to save my friend.

"Wait!" cried Urk.

I ignored him and ran on. With every step, I expected the dragon to burst out from its cave and eat me.

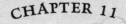

CHAPTER 11

I Do Some Sneaking

The dragon roared. The dragon rumbled.

But it did not leave the cave.

Snatching up Moongobble, I hurried back to the others.

"That was very brave," said the Rusty Knight.

"That was *crazy*," said Urk. "But brave. And we had better not let his mother know about it."

"Never mind that," I said. "How do we turn Moongobble back into himself?"

"We wait," said Urk with a sigh.

"For how long?" asked the Rusty Knight.

Urk shrugged his warty shoulders. "It depends on the spell. Could be an hour. Could be a week. There's no way to tell."

"We can't wait a whole week!" I cried. "Fazwad only gave Moongobble three days to bring him the acorns."

"Can you make the sun rise any faster by telling it you're in a hurry?" asked Urk.

I shook my head.

"Then settle down and wait. If it takes too long, we'll go back so your mother will not worry. Moongobble will have to deal with Fazwad on his own."

"But—"

"Do you have a better idea?" asked Urk. "If not, I am going to take a nap. Wake me when Moongobble turns back into himself." He paused, then added, "Or if the dragon comes out of its cave."

He closed his eyes. A minute later he began to snore.

"I didn't know toads could snore," said the Rusty Knight.

"That toad does a lot of things toads aren't supposed to do," I muttered.

Time went by. Now and then we heard a rumble from the cave. But the dragon did not come out.

The Rusty Knight sat on a tree stump. He did not move, but he did not fall asleep, either. He kept his sword on his knees, ready for action.

I could not sit still. I paced around, feeling nervous and worried. What if Moongobble didn't turn back in time? What if he couldn't be a magician anymore?

It got dark.

The moon rose over the edge of the trees. As the moonlight fell on Moongobble I heard a sound like tinkling bells.

A moment later he turned back into himself.

"Sorry about that," he said, brushing crumbs of cheese off his robe. "Guess I still don't have that spell down right. Anything happen while I was cheesified?"

"Not a thing," I said happily. I went to nudge Urk. "Wake up. He's back!"

Urk jumped in surprise and his eyes flew open. "Well," he said, looking at Moongobble. "Glad to see you. Got any more brilliant ideas?"

Moongobble shook his head.

Urk turned to the Rusty Knight. "How about you?" he yelled.

"How about glue?" asked the Rusty Knight, looking confused.

"*You!*" bellowed Urk. "Do you have any brilliant ideas?"

The Rusty Knight shook his head. "We need to gather more information before I can have a brilliant idea."

"Brilliant!" cried Urk. "Information is just what we need."

"How do we get it?" I asked.

The Rusty Knight put a finger beside his nose. "We must do some spying. Shall I sneak up on the dragon and see what I can learn?"

"You can't sneak up on the dragon," said Urk. "You couldn't sneak up on a tree. You make too much noise. I should do it."

"*You* can't sneak up on the *cave*," said the Rusty Knight. "You don't have a sword. If the dragon sees you, what will you do?"

"Hop away," said Urk.

"You can't hop that fast," I said. Then I took a deep breath and said, "I should be the one to go. I can move very quietly. I can run the fastest. And I have a lot of sneaking practice."

Before they could say no, I scooted away and started toward the cave.

I did not go straight across the clearing. Instead I slipped around the edge of it, staying just inside the ring of trees.

I moved slowly.

I moved silently.

I was more afraid than I wanted to admit.

At last I reached the far side of the clearing.

Dropping to my hands and knees, I crept toward the cave.

Sharp pebbles dug into my hands, but I did not make a sound.

An insect landed on my neck and began to bite

me, but I did not make a sound.

Near the mouth of the cave I dropped flat onto my belly.

Slowly, silently, I pulled myself forward.

Soon I could peer around the rocky wall, into the cave itself.

I gasped in surprise.

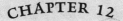

CHAPTER 12

The Dragon of Doom

The dragon was crouched in the center of the cave.

By the moonlight that filtered into the cave I could see him clearly. He had pointy wings. He was covered with red scales. He had sharp fangs.

All that I had expected.

Here is what I had not expected: From his nose to the tip of his tail, the terrible, frightening Dragon of Doom was barely four feet long!

"Go away!" he squeaked, when he saw me looking at him. "Go away!"

I started to laugh. "*You're* the Dragon of Doom?" I asked.

"What's so funny about that?" asked the dragon.

"It's funny because we were all so scared of you," I said. I stood and walked into the cave.

"Who said you could come in?" cried the dragon. "Didn't your mother teach you to knock?"

"Didn't your mother teach you not to frighten people?" I replied. I stopped. The dragon was small, but he might still be dangerous. "How did you make yourself look so big anyway?"

The dragon smiled. "Smoke and mirrors. Fools 'em every time. At least, it did until now. No one has ever been brave enough to sneak up on me like that."

My friends must have gotten worried when they saw me go into the cave, because now they all came running up.

"*You're* the Dragon of Doom?" asked Moongobble.

"We've already been through this," said the dragon. "Yes, *I* am the Dragon of Doom. And yes, I am a little small for the job. And if you want to know where the Golden Acorns are—"

The dragon stopped. He looked sad, and a little scared.

"What?" cried Moongobble. "What is it? Where are they?"

The dragon's head drooped. "I don't know." He sounded as if he were about to cry. "I haven't seen them for years and years."

"Then why are you still guarding the cave?" I asked.

The dragon shrugged his pointy wings. "As long as I keep guarding the cave, people think the acorns are still here. That way no one knows I lost them." He sighed. "It is very shameful to lose a treasure—especially if you are a dragon."

"*Now* what do we do?" I asked.

"We find those acorns!" said Moongobble firmly.

"Do you mind if I come with you?" asked the dragon. "I'd like to know what happened to them myself."

"We don't really

need a dragon on this trip," said Urk.

"Hush!" said Moongobble. "The dragon is perfectly welcome to join us."

"I never thought I'd be traveling with a dragon," said the Rusty Knight. "I was trained to slay them, not make friends with them."

The dragon scurried behind my legs. "Just keep that sword to yourself, buster," he said, spitting a little fire at the Rusty Knight.

"Don't worry," said the Rusty Knight. "I never use my sword on friends."

Moongobble got down on his knees so he could talk to the dragon face to face. "When was the last time you saw the Golden Acorns?" he asked.

The dragon thought. He thought for a long time. He thought so hard smoke came out of his ears.

"Seven years ago," he said at last. "I didn't look at them very often. You couldn't eat them, after all, and I was just supposed to guard them. The last time I saw them was the day I took them out to show to a visitor. The next time I looked, they were gone."

"Who was the visitor?" asked Moongobble.

The dragon shook his scaly little head. "I can't

remember his name. But I do remember what he looked like. He was bald. He had a round face and a pointy nose. And he was very cranky."

"That sounds like Fazwad!" I cried. "But why would Fazwad take the acorns?"

"I don't know," said Moongobble. "But I plan to find out."

It was the first time I ever heard him sound angry.

CHAPTER 13

BACK TO THE COTTAGE

We slept in the dragon's cave that night.

He told me his name was Fireball, and that his entire family had made fun of him because he was so small.

I was starting to think he was kind of cute. Only I didn't say that, because I knew it would insult him.

The next morning we walked back to Pigbone. When we got close to town, Fireball climbed onto my back. He was so small that by clinging to my shoulders, he could stay out of sight of anyone who saw me from the front. We did not want Fazwad to know he was there yet.

Fazwad was waiting at Moongobble's cottage. He smiled when he saw us.

It was not a nice smile.

"Ready to give in, Moongobble?" He sneered.

"I'm ready for the truth," replied Moongobble firmly.

Fazwad looked startled.

"What did you do with the Golden Acorns of Alcoona?" demanded Moongobble.

"What makes you think *I* have them?" asked Fazwad.

"I do!" said Fireball, sticking his head over my shoulder. "You came to my cave and asked to see them. The next time I looked, they were gone! And *you* were the one who took them!"

Fazwad blinked in surprise. "Oh, bat bones! I never expected you to make *friends* with the dragon. I must say, you have done better than I expected, Moongobble."

"But where are my acorns?" demanded Fireball. "Why did you steal them?"

Fazwad reached into his pocket. "I have the acorns right here. And I did not steal them. They belong to the Society of Magicians. The man who was in charge before me was the one who asked you

to guard them. The reason I secretly took them back was to have a good test ready when I needed one." Fazwad turned to Moongobble. "Since you managed to capture the Dragon of Doom, and since the dragon knew who had the acorns, I must admit you have passed this test."

"Thank you," said Moongobble.

The mice in his hat began to cheer.

Moongobble turned to me. "And thank you, Edward. I could not have done it without you."

"What about me?" asked Urk.

"Of course, old friend. I could not have done it without you, either. Or you," he added, turning to the Rusty Knight.

"Spare me the mush," sniffed Fazwad. "Do not forget, you must still perform two more Mighty Tasks before you can join the Society of Magicians."

Moongobble stood up straight and saluted. "I am ready! Tell me what they are!"

Fazwad shook his head. "I did not expect you to pass the first test, so I don't have the next one prepared. But don't worry, I'll have it soon enough.

Trust me, it will not be so easy. In fact, it will be much, *much* harder."

He sniffed twice, then swirled his cloak around him and began to laugh.

An instant later he vanished in a puff of blue smoke.

"What a nasty man," said the Rusty Knight.

Moongobble turned to me. "Edward, if I ever do get to be a full magician, would you like to be my apprentice?"

"And learn real magic?" I cried. "I would love it!"

"Good. Then in reward for your bravery, I think it is time to teach you your first spell. Sort of as a sample of what's to come."

"Uh-oh," muttered Urk. "I'm getting out of here." He hopped away, looking like a frightened mudball.

Fireball fluttered off my shoulder, following Urk.

The Rusty Knight backed around the corner.

Moongobble did not notice. "Watch carefully," he said. Raising his wand, he cried, "Iggle! Biggle! Wotzina Nayme!"

A gust of wind blew past me.

A cloud of green smoke filled the air.

I have to tell you, it was very interesting to be a piece of cheese.

I just hope it never happens again.

About the Author and Illustrator

BRUCE COVILLE is the author of nearly ninety books for young readers, including the international bestseller *My Teacher Is an Alien*. He has been a teacher, a toy maker, a cookware salesman, and a grave digger. In addition to his work as an author, Bruce is much in demand as a speaker and as a storyteller. He is also the founder and president of Full Cast Audio, a company dedicated to producing unabridged recordings of children's books in a full cast format. For more information about Bruce check out www.brucecoville.com.

KATHERINE COVILLE is an artist, sculptor, and doll maker who specializes in highly detailed images of creatures never before seen in this world. She has illustrated several books written by her husband, Bruce Coville, including *Goblins in the Castle, Aliens Ate My Homework,* and the Space Brat Series.

Bruce and Katherine live in Syracuse, New York, with a varying assortment of pets and children.